*This is dedicated to the ones I love.*

To Jack
and
Finley
Love from
Aunty Michelle
x

They get in their boat
and each takes an oar,
Remembering *The Wind
in the Willows* four:
How Ratty and Moley,
Badger and Toad
Lived life on the river
and the open road.

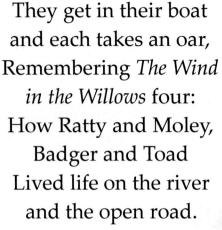

Johnny and Bob,
they like to pretend
That they are these creatures
as they row round the bend.
How eventful and idyllic
their world seemed to be.
"Can we be like that?"
Bob says. "Can we?"

The water is calm,
there's no breeze today.
There are families out
walking and having a play.
The leaves are turning
a yellowy gold.
The days are still warm,
but the evenings are cold.

They get to the bridge where sometimes they meet
With their friends to sit and dangle their feet.
They moor up their boat and trip-trap across,
Over the 'troll', who they both know is Ross.
He always tries to scare them this way.
He does the same thing every single day.
But hold on a second, there's Ross cycling along
the bank of the river, whistling a song.

"So what's under the bridge, shall we take a look?"
"What if it *IS* a troll like we see in our book?"
But they don't like the sounds from below.
So they get in their boat and row, row, row.

"Where are we going, and what if it follows?"
"We'll row so quickly and hide in the hollows!"
They're scared to look back, but curious too...
It's only a boy with nothing to do,
enjoying the echoes his voice is making.
He didn't realise listeners were shaking and quaking!

Up river they row, a little bit wet
From splashing their oars in a hurry, and yet
It doesn't take long to dry out their clothes
In the heat of the sun as they wiggle their toes.

They stop by a tree.
Their legs need a stretch.
A dog is bounding around,
playing catch and fetch.
The tree is horse chestnut,
with spiky green cases.
They're thrilled to find them,
you can see from their faces.
They split open a husk:
a brown conker's revealed!
But Johnny struggles with one,
it's so tightly sealed.

All shiny and polished, there's conkers galore.
"I've found so many, I can't hold any more!"
From his pocket, Bob pulls out two bits of string,
And while threading their conkers, they joyfully sing.
Their game begins and they both want to win.
"Don't hurt my knuckles or damage my skin!"

After a while they call it a draw
And head to their boat.
"What was that I just saw?
There's something hiding
behind that tree.
It throws a huge shadow.
Oh what can it be?"
Bob clings on to Johnny
and holds him so tight.
They don't like this at all,
it just isn't quite right.
The shadow's so large,
and a wolf it resembles!
"Will it gobble us up?"
Bob says as he trembles.

Johnny takes his hand and off they go.
They get in their boat and row, row, row.
"Where are we going and what if it chases?"
"I know where to hide, I know all the best places."
Splashing so fast, away they do flee,
But looking back now, no wolf do they see!
Just a girl playing hide and seek by the tree,
The low sun making her shadow *SO* big, they agree.

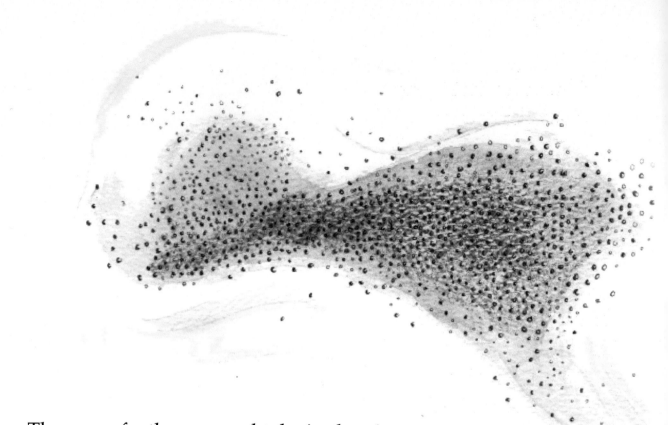

They row further on, and take in the view
Of the autumn leaves and the sky so blue,
Ducks pass by, quacking so loud,
But when they look up, there's a big black cloud.
A strange-looking thing, swirling around.
"It looks so weird, it's making a sound!"
Johnny studies the cloud. He seems to remember
Mum saying you might see this from September.
"It's a murmuration of starlings! It's so cool to see
a reminder of how beautiful nature can be."

They moor up their boat
and take out a bowl.
They're going to fill it to the
brim, that's their goal.
Blackberries are their
favourite, and their
bellies grumble, as they
think of their mum's
homemade crumble.
They race to pick more
than ever before.
There's so many to be found
on the woodland floor,
Then not far away,
they hear a cackle.
"It sounds like a witch I
don't want to tackle!"
And there's more than
one voice – a whole
group of witches.
"I'm very afraid. Shall we
hide in the ditches?"

Johnny grabs Bob. "Come on, let's go"
They get in their boat and row, row, row.
"Where are we going and what if they cast
A spell on us both? We'll have to row fast!"
Safely up river, they look back to see
No witches in sight, just a family
Out picking blackberries, like the two boys
Who mistook their laughter for a cackling noise.

Dad's in his boat, he's been there a while.
Enjoying their antics, he wears a big smile.
Watching his boys, he saw what they could not,
Remembering what scared him when he was a tot.
The boys row back downriver to Dad,
Puffing and panting, happy and glad.
"You've read so many books with baddies and creatures
Scary and hairy with gross gnarly features,
You think that they're real and out to get you,
But they're only in books and are not really true."

They sit still in their boats and start to fish.
"I'm going to get a big one, I wish, I wish."
As Johnny leans over the side he does see
A river monster so big and slimy.
Dad sees it too and now HE's not sure
That these mythical creatures are truly obscure.

They all look again – it's swimming around
Eerily moving, not making a sound.
The water is murky. They start to shiver
At the monster down below in the river.
Johnny leans back. "I'm not staying to know!"
They take their oars and row, row, row.
"Where are we going, how can we escape
From this thing in the water, this horrible shape?"
Dad's still in his boat, trying to see
What has frightened his boys, making them flee.

The figure is rising up from the deep...
It's only Ben cooling down from the heat!
"I've been running around, so hot I was getting
I thought I'd go dipping to help stop me sweating."

They moor up at home and gather their stuff.
Mum says of their blackberries, "That's more than enough!
"I'll be making crumbles and pies forever,
You gathered this many? You boys are so clever!"
"We didn't catch fish though, we had to stop looking!"
Never mind, my dears, it's a roast I am cooking."
A day in the river can be such fun.
I hope you had a good day in the sun."

"We thought we saw witches, wolves, monsters and trolls,
But they were really swans, ducks, herons and voles."
A day on the river is tranquil and bright
If your imagination doesn't give you a fright.
Just before dinner, upstairs they go,
And into the bath they row, row, row.